a minedition book
published by Penguin Young Readers Group

Text copyright © 2004 by Brigitte Weninger
Illustrations copyright © 2004 by Stephanie Roehe
First American edition, 2005
First published in German under the original title:
MIKO „Hurra, Geburtstag!"
translated by Charise Myngheer
Coproduction with Michael Neugebauer Publishing Ltd. Hong Kong.

ISBN 0-698-40015-1

Manufactured in Hong Kong by Wide World Ltd.
Designed by Michael Neugebauer
Typesetting in Kidprint MT
Color separation by Fotoreproduzioni Grafiche, Verona, Italy.
Library of Congress Cataloging-in-Publication Data available upon request.

10 9 8 7 6 5 4 3 2 1
First Impression

Double Birthday! **M**i**KO**

Brigitte Weninger

illustrated by
Stephanie Roehe

minedition

"Wake up Mimiki! Today is the best day ever!
It's my birthday!
There will be pancakes, and I will get lots of presents!"

Mom made Miko's favorite breakfast.

She told him stories about when he was smaller.

"What about Mimiki?" asked Miko. "How old is he?"

"He is exactly as old as you are," answered Mom. "Today is his birthday, too."

"Wow!" said Miko. "A double birthday! But who will give Mimiki presents?" wondered Miko. "I know... I can give him one of mine!"

Mimiki smiled. Miko really was his best friend!

DING-DONG!

The mailman was at the door.

He delivered a present from Grandma
and Grandpa.

"Thank you!" Miko said.

He and Mimiki were both excited.

Miko and Mimiki put the box on the table with the other presents.
"Wow! Look at all of them! I wonder what's inside, don't you?" Miko
whispered into Mimiki's ear.
Mom sang Happy Birthday, and Miko opened his first present.

"Yeah!" shouted Miko.

Grandma and Grandpa sent building blocks!

"We can build a house or an airport!" said Miko.

Mimiki nodded excitedly, but the blocks were too big for his little paws.

"Maybe the next present is a better one for you," said Miko.

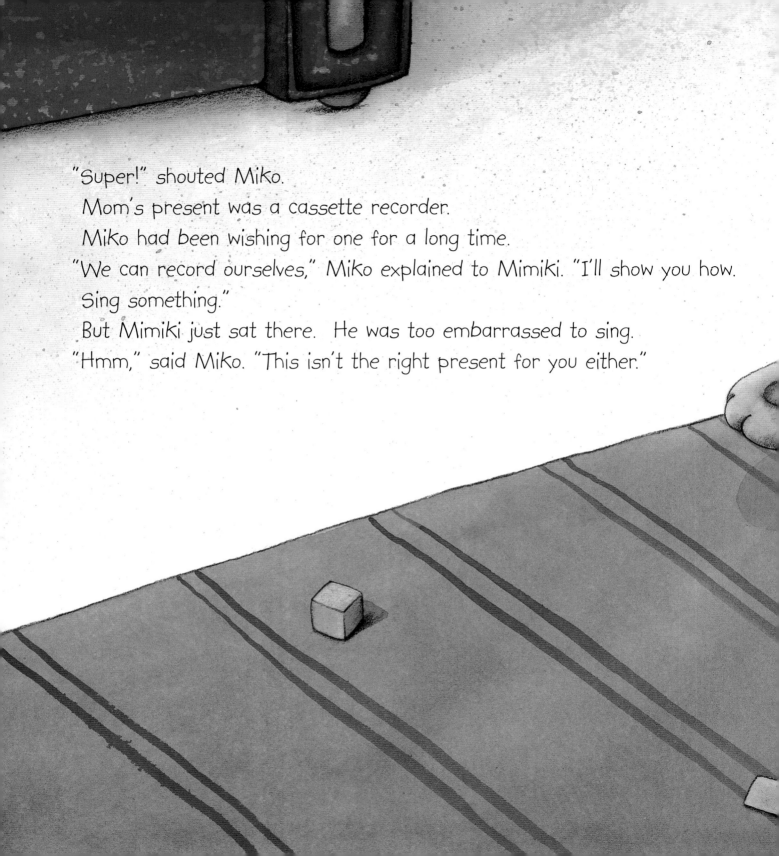

"Super!" shouted Miko.

Mom's present was a cassette recorder.

Miko had been wishing for one for a long time.

"We can record ourselves," Miko explained to Mimiki. "I'll show you how.

Sing something."

But Mimiki just sat there. He was too embarrassed to sing.

"Hmm," said Miko. "This isn't the right present for you either."

The present from Aunt Marie was a picture book. "Look Mimiki. It's the one we saw on TV!"
But, Mimiki couldn't open the book. It was too big. "That's okay," said Miko. "I'll keep this present. Maybe the next one is better for you..."

"Look!
Uncle Max sent a remote control car!
Wow!" Miko tried it out immediately.
"Mimiki, you just press here. Brummm...
then it goes!"
But Mimiki wasn't strong enough to press the button.
"It doesn't matter," comforted Miko. "I can play with it."
Miko steered the car under the table and across the rug.
It was his best birthday ever!

Suddenly, Miko realized that
he was alone.
Where was Mimiki?
It was his birthday, too...

"Oh, no!" realized Miko.
"Mimiki still didn't get
a birthday present!"

Mimiki was sitting on the couch with Mom.
He looked sad.
"What should we do?" asked Miko.
"You can't build things, you can't sing,
you can't turn pages,
and you can't steer.
Not one birthday present was
the perfect one for you..."

Miko thought some more...
"But, Mimiki,"
said Miko suddenly...

"You can live in the house that I build!

And we can listen to
our favorite songs
while we look at
the book together!

You can even ride in
the car. And, I promise
not to steer too fast!"

You know what..."

"We should celebrate our
birthday again!" said Miko.

"Then I can give you half of all of my
presents and we will always play
with them together!
It will be much more fun that way.
Deal?"

Mimiki hugged Miko. "Deal!"

It was the best birthday they ever had!

For more information about MIKO and our other books and the authors and artists who created them, please visit our website: **www.mine**dition.com